Disney
FROZEN
ARENDELLE ADVENTURES
READ-AND-PLAY STORYBOOK

DISNEY PRESS
LOS ANGELES · NEW YORK

CONTENTS

"Across the Sea" written by Brittany Rubiano. Illustrated by the Disney Storybook Art Team.

"Olaf's Perfect Summer Day" written by Jessica Julius. Illustrated by the Disney Storybook Art Team.

"Elsa's Gift" written by Brooke Vitale. Illustrated by the Disney Storybook Art Team.

"Babysitting the Troll Tots" written by Brittany Rubiano. Illustrated by the Disney Storybook Art Team.

For information address Disney Press, 1101 Flower Street, Glendale, California 91201.

Printed in the United States of America
First Edition, July 2015
Library of Congress Catalog Card Number 2015932113
1 3 5 7 9 10 8 6 4 2
G942-9090-6-15163
ISBN 978-1-4847-2389-0

ACROSS THE SEA

"There's our ship, Elsa!" Anna exclaimed, peering out the window. "Are you almost ready?"

"Just about," Elsa replied as she packed the last of her things. She smiled at her sister's impatience, but really, she couldn't wait to go, either.

Elsa had been planning a royal tour to visit nearby kingdoms for a few months. AND NOW IT WAS TIME TO LEAVE! Her heart fluttered with anxious excitement.

As soon as the sisters climbed aboard their ship, the captain scurried over. "Your Majesty," he said to Elsa. "I got the itinerary you sent. But I don't think we'll make it to the first stop on time. Not with waters *this* still."

"DON'T WORRY," ANNA SAID, TAKING THE WHEEL.

"We've got it covered," Elsa said with a smile. "I'll just give us a little nudge." She raised her arms and created a light snow flurry, which helped push the ship along at a steady pace.

"WOO-HOO!" Anna cried from her post, the flurry blowing through her hair. "Away we go!"

Soon the ship arrived at its first port: the kingdom of Zaria. The Zarians clapped and cheered at the sight of their visitors.

"WELCOME, QUEEN ELSA AND PRINCESS ANNA!" King Stebor called in a booming voice.

"We cannot wait to show you our kingdom," Queen Renalia added warmly.

"Thank you!" Anna and Elsa said together, bowing to their hosts.

First the king and queen of Zaria invited the sisters to lunch, where Anna and Elsa enjoyed tasty new foods and lively conversation.

"Renalia thought I couldn't talk when we first met. I was so nervous around her," King Stebor told them.

"OH, THAT'S SWEET!" Anna said.

"Yes, except now he won't stop talking," Queen Renalia joked playfully.

Next Anna and Elsa were taken on a tour of Zaria's prized gardens, where there were many colorful and sweet-smelling blossoms and shrubs on display.

ELSA POINTED OUT A FLOWER THAT LOOKED REMARKABLY LIKE THEIR FRIEND OLAF.

"We'll be sure to send you home with some of those seeds," King Stebor said.

That night, the sisters were treated to a grand festival.

"We've heard so much about your special talents," Queen Renalia said to Elsa. **"WON'T YOU SHOW US SOME OF YOUR MAGIC?"**

Suddenly, Elsa felt very shy. "Would you like to join the dancing, Your Majesties?" she asked, changing the subject. "That looks like fun."

The next morning, the sisters set out for the kingdom of Chatho. The sisters met Chatho's ruler, Queen Colisa, in front of her impressive palace.

"Thank you for having us, Your Majesty," Elsa said.

"Of course," the queen responded. "I AM VERY HAPPY YOU ARE BOTH HERE!"

Queen Colisa first took the sisters on a walk through the kingdom's rainforest, where they saw many unique animals.

Anna was particularly fond of some bashful, furry creatures.

"WHY, HELLO THERE!"

Next the queen led Anna and Elsa into an enormous gallery. Chatho was known for its striking art and relics.

"THESE ARE BEAUTIFUL," Elsa said.

"I'm so glad you think so," Queen Colisa replied. "Would you like to add a sculpture to our collection?"

Suddenly, Elsa noticed a block of ice under a spotlight, ready to be carved. Once again, she felt a wave of shyness.

Noticing her sister's discomfort, Anna jumped in. "UM . . . SURE! ICE SCULPTURES ARE ACTUALLY MY SPECIALTY!"

Later, Anna asked Elsa why she didn't show her powers.

"I guess I just got nervous," Elsa admitted.

Anna smiled. "Well, that's silly. You can do wonderful things." She grabbed some of the snow that had been left by Elsa's snow flurries and placed it on her upper lip. "YOU CAN EVEN GIVE ME A NEW LOOK!"

Elsa laughed and hugged her sister. "Thanks, Anna. You're—"

But Elsa didn't finish her thought. The ship had pulled into their next port, and Elsa had spotted a familiar face: THE DUKE OF WESELTON! This duke had been very unkind to Elsa when her frozen gifts were first revealed.

"What is he doing *here*?" Anna asked. The sisters had purposefully avoided Weselton on their tour. Their last stop before home was the kingdom of Vakretta, far from Weselton.

The Duke smoothed his coat as Anna and Elsa got off the ship. "I am visiting my mother's cousin's wife's nephew if you must know. Although I wish I weren't. If I were you, I WOULD TURN MY SHIP AROUND RIGHT NOW."

The sisters looked at each other.

The Duke sighed, exasperated. "Vakretta has had the hottest summer in years. Of course, you wouldn't care about that."

"Take us to the kingdom," Elsa said firmly.

As the sisters followed the Duke into the village, they noticed Vakrettans sprawled out, sweaty and tired.

"WHOA," Anna remarked.

Elsa didn't feel one bit shy. She knew she had to help cool these folks down. After conjuring some snow clouds, Elsa saw the townsfolk start to come to life.

"It's working!" the Duke cried in surprise.

"Why don't you get us some lemonade?" Elsa prompted the Duke. She started making some frosted mugs out of ice.

"THANK YOU, QUEEN ELSA! THANK YOU!" the crowd cheered.

25

Soon Vakretta became a frozen wonderland. The citizens slid down the snowy piles on wooden planks. Anna grabbed one for Elsa.

"I suppose a thank-you is in order," the Duke said begrudgingly. "I frankly don't know where to begin. . . ."

"Well, you could grab a board," Elsa suggested.

The Duke turned red and started sputtering. "Well . . . a duke would never . . . it isn't . . ."

"IT'S OKAY. WE'LL SHOW YOU HOW IT'S DONE," ANNA CALLED, RACING HER SISTER UP THE HILL.

A few hours later, it was time for Anna and Elsa to return to Arendelle. They waved to their new friends from the ship.

"Did you have a good trip?" Anna asked her sister.

"I did," Elsa replied as she created a blast of snow flurries to direct them homeward. "I'd say that was the best royal tour ever . . . UNTIL NEXT TIME, THAT IS!"

OLAF'S PERFECT SUMMER DAY

Summer had finally arrived in Arendelle. Everyone in the kingdom was enjoying the long, sunny days after a very cold winter season.

THIS WAS GOING TO BE THE HOTTEST DAY OF THE YEAR SO FAR!

Most of the villagers wanted to stay inside, where it was cool, but Olaf could hardly wait to get outside! THIS WAS THE KIND OF DAY HE HAD ALWAYS DREAMED ABOUT!

Olaf ran into Princess Anna's room.

"Anna! Anna!" he called. "Guess what today is? IT'S THE PERFECT SUMMER DAY! Let's go outside and play!"

Anna groaned as she sat up in bed. "It's so hot and sticky, Olaf," she said. But she had to smile when she saw Olaf's hopeful face.

Together, Olaf and Anna went to look for Queen Elsa. They found her in the Great Hall.

"THERE YOU ARE, ELSA!" Olaf cried out joyfully.

Olaf looked up shyly at the dignitary standing with Elsa. "Hi, my name is Olaf, and I like warm hugs."

"H-h-hello," the dignitary stammered in surprise. He had never seen a talking snowman before.

Olaf turned back to Elsa. "And today is the best day for warm hugs, because it's sunny and hot. PLEASE, CAN WE GO PLAY IN THE SUNSHINE?"

Elsa laughed. "That sounds like fun, Olaf. What did you have in mind?"

"It's so hot, though. Couldn't you cool things down just a bit, Elsa?" Anna looked hopefully at her sister.

"Olaf's always wanted to experience heat. Shouldn't we give him his special day? WE'LL DO EVERYTHING HE'S ALWAYS WANTED TO DO IN SUMMER!"

"You're right, Elsa," agreed Anna. "How about a picnic on the shores of the fjord?"

Olaf clasped his hands with glee. "Oooo, I love picnics!"

Anna, Elsa, and Olaf
trooped to the royal kitchens for
picnic supplies. They found Olina with her
head in the icebox.

"OLINA, WHAT ON EARTH ARE YOU DOING?" asked Elsa.

Olina popped her head up. "Trying to keep myself cool. It's so terribly hot!"

Olaf giggled. "Did you bake cookies today?"

Olina shook her head. "Oh, it's much too hot for baking."

Elsa glanced at Olaf. She didn't want to disappoint him. "How about an ice-cold lemonade instead?" she suggested.

Olaf was thrilled. "OOOO, I LOVE LEMONADE!"

Olaf, Anna, and Elsa set off for their picnic adventure.

At the royal gardens, a few children were lying on the field, too hot to play games. But Olaf didn't notice. Giggling delightedly, he ran to them.

"HI, MY NAME IS OLAF. DON'T YOU JUST LOVE SUMMER?" The children, charmed by Olaf, joined him in chasing butterflies and blowing fuzz off the dandelions.

Even Elsa and Anna couldn't resist joining in.

After a while, Anna plopped down on the grass. "Whew! I'm ready for our picnic!"

Elsa agreed. "Yes, let's head to the docks. WE CAN SAIL TO THE FJORD."

Olaf, who had been chasing a bumblebee, stopped in his tracks. "We're going sailing? I've always wanted to try sailing!"

At the docks, Anna and Elsa chose a beautiful sailboat. As they set sail, OLAF HUMMED HAPPILY.

When they reached the shore, Elsa set up the picnic blanket. But Olaf couldn't sit still. "Don't you just love the feeling of sand on your snow, Anna?" he squealed. "LET'S MAKE SAND ANGELS TOGETHER!"

Anna gingerly stuck a toe in the sand. "Oh, goodness, that is . . . uh . . . warm," she squeaked.

She danced on tiptoe over to the fjord's edge. "AH, THIS IS BETTER," she said as water washed over her feet.

The three friends spent the whole
afternoon PLAYING IN THE SUMMER SUN.
They built sand
castles and sand people.

They **CHASED WAVES**
on the shore.

They even **DANCED**
WITH SEAGULLS.

Finally, when they'd tired themselves out, Anna, Elsa, and Olaf had a picnic on the shores of the fjord.

"HANDS DOWN, THIS IS THE BEST DAY OF MY LIFE," said Olaf.

As they sailed back to Arendelle, the setting sun made beautiful colors in the sky. OLAF WAS AMAZED. "I wish I could hug the summer sun. I bet it would feel wonderful!"

Anna smiled as she pushed her sweaty hair off her face. "You might need a bigger snow flurry for that, Olaf."

Back at the docks, Kristoff and Sven were waiting. They had spent the afternoon harvesting mountain lakes. Now their sled was full of ice.

Jumping out of the boat, Anna flung herself on the delicious cold blocks. "OH, AM I GLAD TO SEE YOU!"

Olaf told Kristoff and Sven all about his adventures. "I wish it could always be summer!" he said.

"Summer is wonderful," Elsa agreed, smiling at Anna's antics. "BUT TOMORROW, I PREDICT A CHANCE OF SNOW."

ELSA'S GIFT

Snow fell quietly on the kingdom of Arendelle. Snowflakes tickled children's noses and melted on their tongues. The people of Arendelle waded through deep, powdery snowdrifts as they hurried through the streets. Everyone welcomed the snow, for this time it was not Queen Elsa's doing. IT WAS WINTER!

Inside the castle, Queen Elsa and Princess Anna watched their subjects bustle to and fro. Everyone was preparing for the winter ball Elsa was throwing that evening.

ELSA SMILED. For the first time since she was a child, the kingdom's gates were open. Elsa's ice magic was finally under control. And most important, SHE AND HER SISTER WERE FRIENDS AGAIN.

Anna grabbed Elsa's arm and dragged her away from the window. "Come on!" she said. "WE HAVE SO MUCH TO DO TO GET READY FOR THE BALL!"

Elsa chuckled and let herself be pulled. Anna was right. There *was* a lot to do!

Anna and Elsa had been hard at work for days. Decorations hung from every wall, and the castle glittered with Elsa's frosty magic. But there were still some finishing touches to add.

While Elsa finished icing the banquet room, Anna raced to the kitchens. "There," she said, coming back into the room with a tray full of *krumkake*. "The dessert table is ready! WHAT DO YOU THINK, ELSA?"

But Elsa wasn't paying attention.

"EARTH TO ELSA," Anna called.

Elsa looked at her sister and smiled. Anna's act of love had saved Arendelle—and Elsa. Elsa wanted to do something to show everyone how much she loved her sister.

Looking around the banquet room, Elsa had an idea. "I, um . . . I have to go," she told Anna.

Elsa raced out the door . . . and almost ran right into Olaf!

"Hi, Elsa," Olaf said. "Where are you going?"

"To the kitchen," Elsa said. "I'm going to make cookies for Anna. Do you want to help?"

Olaf clapped his hands. "I love cookies!"

The pair headed to the kitchen and shut themselves inside. They had just started getting ingredients together when Anna knocked on the door. "Elsa? Are you in there?" she called.

"Don't come in!" Elsa said. "YOU'LL RUIN THE SURPRISE!"

Elsa and Olaf waited until they heard Anna walk away. Then they finished gathering ingredients.

"You know," Elsa said to the snowman, "I DON'T THINK YOU SHOULD GO ANYWHERE NEAR AN OVEN."

"Pshaw!" Olaf exclaimed, waving his twiggy arms. "WHAT COULD POSSIBLY GO WRONG?"

Soon the two were busy making extra-gingery gingerbread men—Anna's favorite. The cookies turned out perfectly, and Elsa only had to refreeze Olaf seven times!

Next Elsa decided to make Anna's favorite punch. She was stirring the punch when Anna walked into the kitchen.

"You can't be in here!" Elsa exclaimed. "I'm working on your surprise."

"I just want to—" Anna started, but Elsa cut her off.

"Just go to your room, Anna," Elsa said, turning her back on her sister. "I'll see you later."

Anna left, and Elsa finished making the punch. Then she went back to the banquet room Everything looked beautiful, but there was nothing special. Elsa thought for a minute. Then, waving her hands, she created a glittering ice sculpture of Anna.

Just then, Kristoff came into the room. "I just saw Anna in the courtyard," he told Elsa. "She said you told her to go away! She seems upset."

"Oh, no! I didn't mean to hurt her feelings," Elsa said. "I just didn't want her to ruin her surprise!"

"You know, I think what she would really like is just to spend time with her big sister. YOU SHOULD GO TALK TO HER," Kristoff suggested.

Elsa rushed into the snowy courtyard. "ANNA? WHERE ARE YOU?" she called, looking around. "Please come out. I'm so sorry, Anna, I just—"
SPLAT! A snowball hit Elsa right in the face.
"Surprise!" Anna yelled, jumping out from behind a tree.

"W-what?" Elsa sputtered, brushing the snow off her face. "Did you just—?"
Anna giggled. "It's a snowball intervention, Elsa," she said dramatically.
"Since you don't seem to have any time for me, I'M DECLARING WAR! I knew
Kristoff could get you out here!"

Elsa started to grin. "Anna," she said. "I think you're forgetting which one of us has magical ice powers." She made a huge snowball and hurled it at Anna. But Anna was ready for her. SHE HAD PREPARED A WHOLE PILE OF SNOWBALLS!

The snowball fight went on and on, until at last Elsa called a truce. It was time for the sisters to get ready for the ball! Elsa glanced slyly at Anna. Then, hurling one final snowball at her sister, she raced inside. "GOTCHA!" she cried.

That night, the sisters greeted their guests. As Anna looked around the banquet room, she noticed Elsa's cookies and punch and her beautiful sculpture.

"You did this for me?" she said.

Elsa nodded. "I wanted to give you a perfect gift," she said.

"It's all lovely," Anna said. "And it was very sweet of you. But for me, THE BEST PRESENT EVER IS JUST BEING WITH YOU."

"For me, too," Elsa said. And linking arms, the sisters went off to enjoy their party . . . together.

Babysitting the Troll Tots

Anna pulled on her boots. Her friends Kristoff and Sven would be there any minute. It was a beautiful spring evening, and they were going to watch over the toddler trolls while the adults went to their annual magical prophesying convention.

"Are you sure you don't need me to come?" Elsa asked. "I can provide some magical help."

"I think we've got it covered," Anna said, giving her sister a quick hug. "They're just babies. HOW HARD COULD IT BE?"

Soon Anna, Kristoff, and Sven set off. As they rode to the trolls' valley, Kristoff told Anna stories about growing up with the sweet and silly creatures.

"I wonder if I should have brought games," Anna said. "DO TROLLS LIKE GAMES?"

"Oh, don't worry," Kristoff responded. "THEY'LL PROBABLY SLEEP THE WHOLE TIME. I BET WE'LL BE RELAXING BY THE FIRE. MAYBE EATING SOME SNACKS."

He explained that Bulda, his adopted mother, set a very strict bedtime for all the young trolls. Sven grunted in agreement.

As Anna, Kristoff, and Sven entered the valley, dozens of mossy rocks rolled toward them. SUDDENLY, THE TROLLS APPEARED AND A CHORUS OF GREETINGS ERUPTED.

"Kristoff! Sven! Anna! Welcome! We missed you!"

Bulda looked Kristoff over. "It seems like just yesterday *you* were young enough to have a sitter," she said.

"Remember when all he wanted to do was run naked through the valley?" Grand Pabbie asked.

"Oh, really?" Anna asked, stifling a giggle. "You never mentioned *that*."

"Okay, that's enough stories for now," Kristoff said.

Bulda led Anna and Kristoff to the troll tots. "If they get
hungry, you can feed them smashed berries. And they may need
a leaf change. BUT IT'S JUST ABOUT THEIR BEDTIME, SO THEY SHOULD BE
SLEEPING SOON."

As the adult trolls headed off, Anna waved. "Have a great time!
Everything is going to be . . ."

"A DISASTER!" she finished.

The toddler trolls had escaped from their pen when no one was looking. NOW THEY WERE RUNNING, CLIMBING, AND SWINGING ALL OVER THE PLACE.

"Oh . . . no, no," Anna said, rushing to help a few trolls who were climbing up the boulders. "That's dangerous."

Kristoff ran to a leaning tower of trolls that had sprouted.

"All right, guys," Kristoff said, gently pulling the trolls off one another. "LET'S SETTLE DOWN NOW."

But the more Kristoff, Anna, and Sven tried to calm the little trolls, THE WILDER THEY BECAME.

"Maybe they're hungry!" Anna said, heading for the basket of smashed berries.

"YUMMY!" she cooed, offering one of the toddlers a spoonful of berries. But the trolls clearly felt they had better things to do.

"Maybe they need changing," Kristoff said. He bravely peered into one of the trolls' nappy leaves. "Nope."

"Let's put them to bed," Anna suggested. "They must be tired by now."

But alas, THE YOUNG TROLLS WERE WIDE AWAKE.

Suddenly, a cheery voice interrupted them.
"HELLO, TROLL BABIES!"
It was their friend Olaf!

"Elsa sent me in case you needed some help," Olaf explained, turning to the trolls. "WHY, HI, THERE. HA-HA! THAT TICKLES!"

"Boy, are we glad to see you," Kristoff said.

Anna ran to greet the snowman. But in her hurry, she
tripped and fell face-first into the
basket of berries!

"WHOAAA!"

Kristoff rushed to her side.
"Anna! Are you okay?"

Anna lifted her head. HER FACE WAS COVERED IN DRIPPING PURPLE GOOP.

The little trolls burst into loud giggles. They stampeded toward her and LAPPED UP THE BERRY JUICE ON HER CHEEKS.

Anna laughed. "Well, I guess that's one way to feed them."

AFTER THE TROLLS WERE DONE, THEY SAT IN A HEAP, HAPPY AND FULL. Suddenly, a strange smell floated through the air. The trolls looked down at their leaves.

"Uh-oh," Kristoff said knowingly. "Olaf, you distract them."

Olaf told the little trolls a story while Anna and Sven collected leaves and Kristoff changed diapers. SOON EVERYONE WAS CLEAN AND SWEET-SMELLING ONCE MORE.

"And now for a showstopping song!" Olaf announced.

Anna noticed that the trolls were swaying. Some of them were having trouble keeping their eyes open.

"Actually," she said, "maybe Kristoff and Sven would like to sing a lullaby instead."

"Good thing I brought my lute," Kristoff replied while Anna and Olaf began putting the trolls to bed.

"ROCK-A-BYE TROLL-YS, IN YOUR SMALL PEN," Kristoff sang.

"Time to go sleepy for Uncle Sven," Kristoff as Sven crooned.

By the time the adult trolls returned, the toddlers were sound asleep.

"Wow, great job," Bulda whispered.

"It was easy," Anna replied, elbowing Kristoff.

"Piece of mud pie," Kristoff added.

Bulda smiled and hugged her friends. "YOU TWO WILL BE GREAT PARENTS SOMEDAY!"